THE UNTOLD SECRETS

SOHAM GUPTA

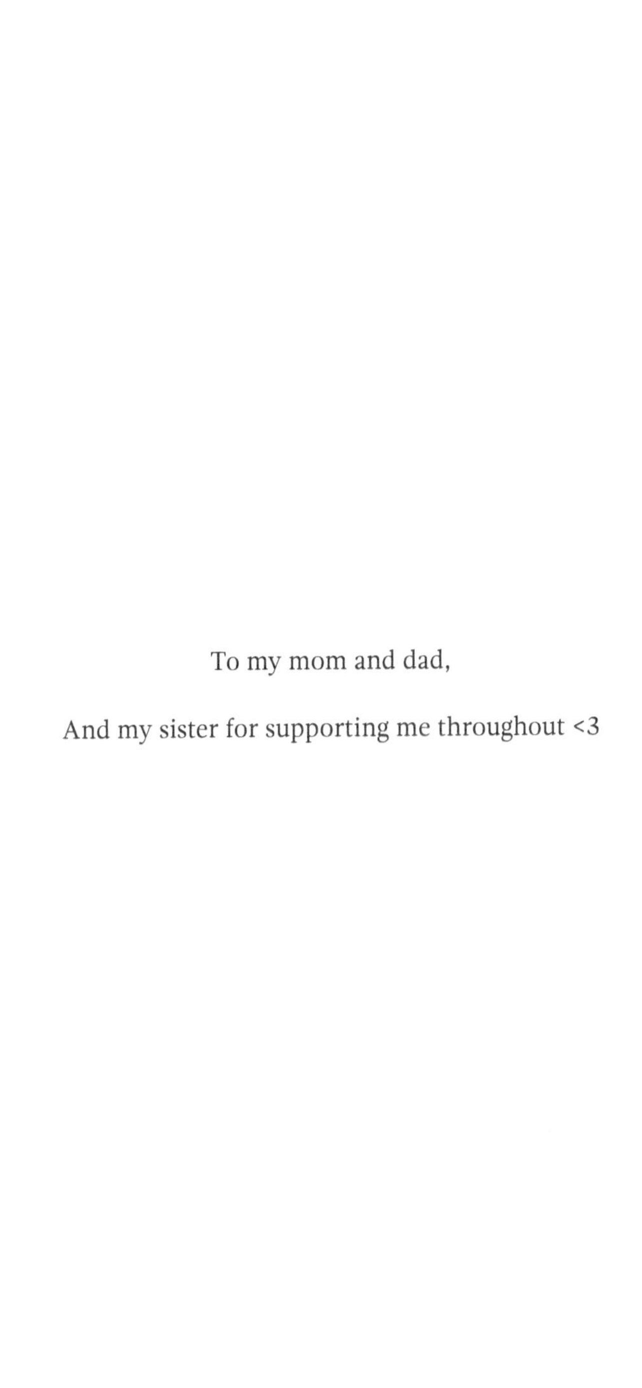

To my mom and dad,

And my sister for supporting me throughout <3

Contents

Foreword

Even if things make sense, it doesn't mean it's true, If you
believe so,
Be prepared to be proved wrong.

Preface

After a few hours, they entered the living room and sat at the dining table. No one was ready to talk about what happened, however knowing that it had to be touched upon, Rovendy said, "I was thinking something about the note he gave us. It reminds me of something. Isabella, could you pass me the Fineominetic history book from school?" She nodded and passed it to him. He flipped through the pages and stopped on page 234. He read aloud, "People believe that Sachel Salegio passed a chit to a mysterious man after she went into hiding. It is said to contain a clue to an upcoming disaster's solution in the coming years. The one being a person's plot of destruction." They all saw this very text written in the book. Isabella announced in disbelief, "The driver... it's him. He knows something. It's a myth worthy of being checked out. If he can lead us to Sachel, she could give us a heads up, or maybe a solution or something to stop Aladana and our parents." Myran suggested, "We should probably meet with this guy to coax information. Anyone got his contact?" They all shook their heads.

Surlay took the chit and discovered a number at the back of it. He dialled it on the telephone. It was the driver. Surlay said with confidence and a pinch of nervousness, "We know who you are. Come pick us up at our place tomorrow morning at ten." The driver disconnected. They took that as a yes.

Just as Myran was going back to the couch, the telephone started ringing. Isabella raised an eyebrow and picked up, "Hello, this is the Novinsk Residence speaking." A screechy voice replied, "Quit the formal talk. This is

Sachel. I see you know about my little friend. The stories are true... most of them at least. Anyway, he told me that you wanted to talk. Probably to get to talk to me. So we are gonna do this according to my time convenience. Today at six PM. Don't be late. I don't treat my guests well if they're late. My friend is coming to pick you up. Any changes I'll let you know." Isabella took a deep breath. She narrated the whole story. They all were in awe. Meanwhile, Rovendy reminded them, "That is in two hours. We better get ready!" They all rushed into their respective bedrooms to change.

Vovolint City

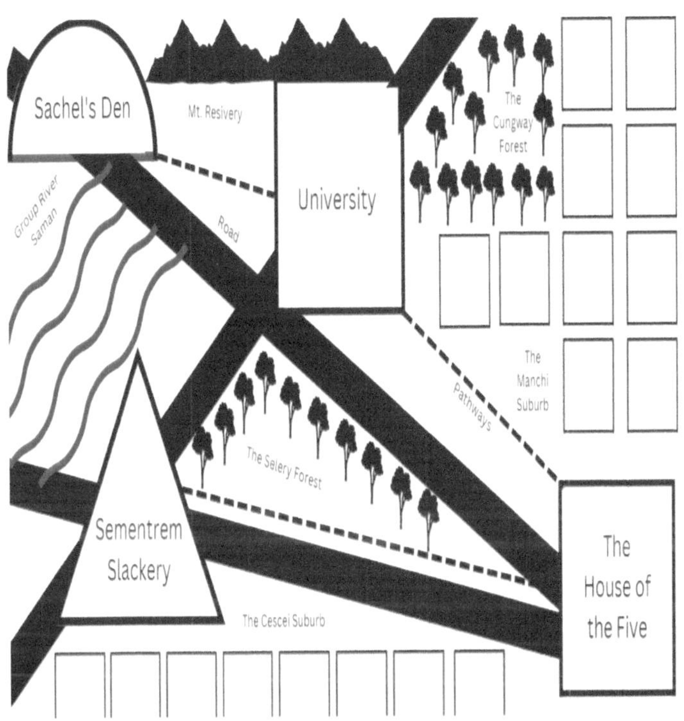

CHAPTER ONE

THE NOVINSK PROTECTORS

A massive spaceship hovered in the air. Thin, robot-like arms stretched out, ready to capture any target. The sky turned blood red, as evil vibes spread throughout. Down below on the earth's surface, preparations commenced. For the past few years, the family of Dramatus has been protecting the earth from all the dangers. They were mysterious aliens from a distant planet but no one knew why they chose to protect humans on Earth. However, critics pointed out that attacks on Earth from external planets had increased since the Dramatus's arrival. Nonetheless, they continued serving Earth for the better.

Each of them possessed a unique ability, which no other being possessed as far as human knowledge was concerned. Isabella was a hyndofine. She could control, produce and attack with water. She was gorgeous. Her hair was a perfect blend of dark navy blue and pitch black. Her skin was milky white and she had turquoise eyes. Her elegant blue robes highlighted her dainty features. However, she had immense power that no one would dare to doubt.

Rovendy was a fineomine. He could harness fire. He could do anything with fire, from setting a city ablaze to lighting the tiniest bonfires. He had fiery eyes, and a staff that he used in a one-on-one fight. He had a blood-red gown with a bold, mature look on his face.

Surlay was a thunfand. He could control and unleash thunder. Contrary to his powerful ability, he was compassionate by nature. Since his arrival thunderstorms were daily occurrences in many areas. He was the most handsome of them all with blonde hairs, big round eyes and a small mouth.

The Mylia Twins were certainly the most powerful of the five. Myran could control light, giving him the power to annoy squirrels with his powers, which he loved. Mifina could control darkness and shadows. She had soft features with hazel-like skin. Myran wore a white cape while Mifina wore black. They even dyed their hair differently according to their powers.

Panic was striking everywhere: on every corner of the globe. The machine arms had already come in sight. The Great Guardians - as they were popularly known - were getting ready for possibly the biggest battle they had ever faced. A person in one of the spaceship hoisted a red flag, dangling halfway midair from the spaceship. With the help of a powerful microphone, he demanded that the five teens had to surrender to them, or else they would have to be taken by force. Luckily, the five always had a plan for these unforeseen situations. Their tactic was to play defence. They would remain out of the enemy's sight and attack at random from any location causing maximal damage. Seeing that the Great Guardians were not co-orperating, he decided to push forward. As the flying spaceship appeared in the range, the army, navy and the Airforce launched their weapons. Nothing happened. The spaceship continued drifting at a faster speed. Finally, the five heroes sprang into action.

Isabella created a huge water tornado while Rovendy created multiple fire rings stacked one on top of the other. Surlay sent huge blasts of lightning which smashed into the spaceships causing only a few dents. The Mylia Twins too sprinted into action. Mifina wrapped the ships in darkness causing them to collide with one another, while Myran sent a thread of light - that penetrated through the spaceships- wreaking havoc.

However, the sides changed all too quickly. All the heroes vanished as the spaceship disappeared. The crowd gasped, praying for their heroes' return. But what had happened? This event wasn't a coincidence. It was planned, perfected and implemented.

CHAPTER TWO

A WHOLE NEW WORLD

Time flew by swiftly just like a falcon diving for its prey. The GG woke up slowly, as their eyes adjusted to the light - except for Myran, who immediately got up. They were surrounded by metal bars- around three feet wide. They had to try to break out. All of them tried shooting with the help of their powers at the bars. However, as soon as their power struck the bars, it immediately ricocheted back at them. Confidently, Miffina asked them to stand back and pointed that the bars were made of iron, and so she could corrode them. However, her thoughtful plan went in vain. Despite numerous attempts, she couldn't corrode the jail. She later on went to discover, that it was an alloy, so her plan was doomed from the start. It was as if the enemy was prepared for what they had in stock.

At the worst time possible, Surlay became emotional and sobbed saying that they would never be able to get out of that place because it was a nightmare. Rovendy screamed at Surlay to shut up so he followed his command. They needed to strategize and plan their attack. They all knew that the first thing to do was to gather information about the people who had trapped them in that madness.

A guard approached their prison cell and offered some food to them. Isabelle took the lead and gave the guard a stern look. The guard was scared, dropped the food and quickly ran away. Rovendy sniffed the food to determine if it was safe to consume and thankfully it was. So he took a bite and looked ecstatic. He proclaimed that it was the best thing he had ever eaten. The guard returned and confidently stated that Fineomines cannot resist the delicious taste of cheese-infused Rendomeys. All of them looked at the guard with open mouths in disbelief.

"You see, you guys aren't the only ones who have these abilities. There is a whole planet of people with special abilities like yours. I have come on a mission to rescue you from the horror of humans. Will you come home?" an unknown voice spoke and before they could utter a single word, they were suffocated in a tiny bag where their powers didn't work at all. They were frustrated by being transported against their will to unknown places. Right after a few seconds, they were teleported to another place.

They managed to get out of the bags and what they saw next left them awestruck. They were in the middle of a lavish house. It had a double ceiling, ornated walls, top-of-the-line luxury products, and more than enough areas and equipment to practice and enhance their abilities. A scrawny lady appeared out of the blue and said, "This is your new home. Luckily enough, we were able to retrieve you in time just for your first day in Ability College. Each ability has a different wing. It is situated downtown and within walking distance. It starts in two hours. Do not be late." And just like that she disappeared.

A bunch of clothes with name tags were stacked neatly on a counter in front of them, along with the notebooks and pens. Isabelle had to wear an ice-blue uniform with the tag 'JUNIOR HYNDOFINE' imprinted on it. In the same way, everyone had their uniforms in their respective colours with all of them being juniors. They picked up their respective stuff, quickly claimed their rooms, got changed and headed off to what might be the biggest change in their life. They had to get to know this whole place to which they were brought.

They left the extravagant house and headed to the college. As they approached closer to the college, they realised it wasn't like anything they had ever set their eyes on before. The massive intricate gate guarded the towering buildings like a dog. The college comprised of a big main tower with a crown like dome that pierced the sky. Next to it were modernised glass towers connected by a wooden bridge that came straight from the woods. There were five towers – each specially designed and engineered for its respective ability. It was like they were enveloped in its beauty. Taking a deep breath, they passed through the gate and entered the main building wondering what lurked behind those doors.

CHAPTER THREE

An Influx Of Information

The bells echoed throughout the halls signalling the start of the lectures. The five of them had no idea where to go. Luckily, no one knew the way as it was the first day of the term. Teachers came and led each of them in their respective classrooms.

After thirty minutes, the lectures commenced. Excited whispers echoed through the long hallways. After a few study hours, it was lunchtime. All the students had to proceed to the dining hall. All five of them sat at a table far more secluded than the others. Isabella started explaining about the history of Hyndofines as it was told during her class. Rovendy had the same account. Myran fell asleep halfway through the conversation and so did Surlay. Mifina seemed excited after her session as they got to do some practical work.

Just as everyone was going to proceed to the next lectures, the headmistress - Miss Aladana - announced, "Sorry for the inconvenience but the school will close early today right after lunch. Now pack your bags, chop-chop. I want everyone out in ten minutes apart from Isabella

Fonx, Rovendy Artrem, Miffina and Myran Sean, and Surlay Haffer. These five please report to my office now. I will be there in a few minutes".

None of them believed in coincidences and rightfully so. What were the chances that the principal would call five new people who came from this entire world's arch-nemesis on the first day of the term? Not likely. Surrounded with questions, they marched into the esteemed office. It was as if they were entering the magical land. Anyone's eyes could go blind after looking at all the crystals of this sparkly room reflecting all the light. They sat on the chairs that lay empty in front of them- diamond made and a pearl-outlined desk.

After a few minutes, Miss Aladana entered the room. Comfortably, she sat down on her leather enfolded seat. She informed them that their arrival had caused some concern in their world. She mentioned that although the teens were one of them, they could not be certain where kids' loyalties lied due to the fact the five of them had spent a significant amount of time around humans. Aladana also stated that they were under strict orders from The Board Of Mysains to keep a close eye on them and assess whether they were worthy of staying. She warned the five of them that if they were not deemed worthy, banishment would be the only option and that they would be under observation for six months for the same purpose. She warned them not to attempt to escape as there was high-level security in place and advised them to approach her if they had any issues and then dismissed them. The five of them did as told and returned to their new home.

All of them collapsed on the bed as the day was far more exhausting than they hoped it would be, except the Mylia Twins. They were quite well known for their intellectual deviousness. This also brought about lots and lots of energy in them. So, they were jumping all around. Surlay suggested, "Why don't you both make use of your energy and probably you know, TRAIN!" They both chuckled and said, "Training is for losers." Surlay rolled his cute eyeballs but right in the next second, he put on his really serious face, which was quite intimidating.

Feeling cowed, the Mylia Twins rushed off to the training grounds. Rovendy said, "I guess we should also do some training. It might divert us. Moreover, we haven't even checked out the new grounds. I bet it's filled with lots of cool stuff." The others gave a forceful nod and went to the training ground. What they set their eyes on next, was a miracle and a dream fulfilled.

The Mylia Twins were already excited to share some exciting news. Isabella asked them to spill the details. Myran said they had explored the whole area and found something amazing. Miffina explained that there was a big screen which served as a leaderboard. She added that they had to participate in a face-off every month and the screen would record the scores, giving ranks from one to five. She also mentioned that there was a tournament every three months with the winner getting to choose whatever winner wanted for the entire day. Surlay suggested that they start the next day for the first fight of the month and they all agreed. Isabella then instructed the twins to enter their names and powers to begin the fun. Fast enough, the next day started.

The Mylia Twins eagerly entered their names and powers into the system, ready to compete and see where they ranked on the leaderboard. Isabella, Miffina, Myran, and Surlay all felt a surge of adrenaline as they prepared themselves for the first face-off of the month. As the day of the competition arrived, the Mylia Twins met together at the designated area, surrounded by other participants who were also vying for the top spots on the leaderboard.

The tension in the air was palpable as they waited for the signal. The face-off began, and the twins used their powers, outmanoeuvring and outsmarting their opponents. In a flurry of action and strategy, they fought fiercely, determined to prove themselves and climb the ranks. After the dust settled and the scores were tallied, the leaderboard displayed the results.

The Mylia Twins were thrilled to see that they had all achieved high ranks, and especially ecstatic that they won. They celebrated their success and looked forward to the next tournament, where they would have the chance to win another day of their choosing. In the meanwhile though, they ordered that everyone except them had to wear their socks on their hands the whole day. The rest of them groaned.

The Mylia Twins were proud of their achievements and grateful for the exciting opportunity to compete in the face-offs and tournaments. They knew that with determination, teamwork and dedication, they could continue to rise through the ranks and become champions in the world of competitive gaming. Many hours passed by and the nightfall approached. They all hit the sack early, excited to see what the next day had in store for them. Rovendy, however wasn't in the right mind to sleep. He kept wondering if there was something fishy. Nevertheless, he wasn't going to let this thought sabotage their fun which was much awaited. All of them caught some heavy Z's waiting for the night to pass.

CHAPTER FOUR

A Bucket Of Secrets

Dawn broke with a light gradient of pink and orange in the sky. As expected, the Mylia Twins were the first to get up and knock at everyone's door to remind them of how much energy they had to muster. By 7 a.m., everyone was up and ready, and they all met at the training grounds, where the Mylia Twins were both the hosts and participants, of course. Everybody sat on the side chairs next to the fighting stage. Myran announced that the first battle was between Miffina and Isabella and he encouraged everyone to get ready for a serious match. After requesting the two girls to go, Myran jumped off the stage to join the audience and watched as the match began.

No one knew who was stronger, which was probably why Myran picked the two of them to fight first. Miffina threw a shadow rope at Isabella but she countered it with a water shield. Isabella then retaliated with a massive water meteor, which Miffina was able to reflect using a dark mirror causing it to crash down on Isabella. Myran announced a point to Mifinna while observing Isabella's current state of anger.

As the rounds progressed, both girls continued to claim victories alternatively. Finally, after hours of fighting, they both hesitantly nodded and stepped down from the stage as none of them seemed to be winning. As Myran began to introduce the next match, Rovendy interjected expressing exhaustion and suggesting they continue the competition the following day.

None of them except Surlay seemed to be tired. It was quite strange considering that the competition had just started. They offered Surlay to withdraw for day, reminding him that he would most surely come last. Shrugging his shoulders, he offered to be a referee and host, so that the Mylia Twins could also join the fun. Without wasting a second, Myran and Miffina handed him the sheets, and sat with the other contestants.

Surlay called on the much-awaited fight of the twins versus Rovendy. Myran and Miffina wanted to be on the same team, so they agreed to fight alternatively in order to ensure the integrity of the tournament. However, they couldn't help but cheat. However they did it discreetly. While Myran was fighting Rovendy, Miffina helped enhancing her brother's powers, making sure she wasn't seen. Like this, they defeated all their opponents, which took quite some time.

By the time the scores were tallied, the sun started setting. It seemed as though the Mylia Twins won. They celebrated like wild chickens. Mischievous by nature, they ordered the rest three of them to wear socks on their hands for the rest of the day. A moan roared in the twins' ears.

They decided to head back home after an exhausting day. Upon reaching the house, Surlay voiced his suspicions about the situation feeling that there was more to Miss Aladana's story than she was letting on. The others agreed.

They were determined to squeeze out information from Miss A and discreetly uncover the truth.

They all decided to order some food, as they were famished. Within an hour, it came. It was already late and so they quickly gulped up the food and headed to bed. It had just been ten minutes and suddenly the doorbell rang. Miffina asked, "Who could be there at this hour? We didn't order any extra food, did we?" Rovendy shook his head. Myran bolted to the door and wrenched it open.

Myran stood frozen. They all tried to take a sneak peek at who had just mysteriously arrived. He looked just like Miffina, the same tanned skin, the jet-black hair... Right next to the man popped a woman who was just like Myran, skin as white as milk and cotton-like hair. They said, "I know Myran you must be thinking a billion things... You too Miffina. How do we know your names? Why do we look so alike to each other? What's up with all the similarities? All will be revealed. First, if you would be so kind to let us in. It is freezing outside." Myran stepped aside while Isabella and Rovendy led them to the lounge room. They took a seat and everyone was shocked at the turn of the events one after the other.

A few moments passed as everyone settled down into their favourite chairs. Surlay made some coffee and served everyone. Miffina and Myran demanded, "Now, we want some explanations. Start talking."

CHAPTER FIVE

THE MIRACLE

The two uninvited guests explained that they were not sure how to put it clearly, but they were their parents with the names Selorafe Feal and Kintentia Feal. The Mylia Twins were about to interrupt but their parents gestured them to stop with their raised hands. The supposed father admitted that he understood how it all seemed very confusing and proceeded to explain that all of them, including the twins, were born on the planet. Life was perfect there until it took a dark turn when a group of people called the Antminales opposed the government and started a civil war. The majority of the inhabitants had to flee the planet in spaceships, similar to the ones that were sent to get the twins. Each spaceship had a tracker intended to bring the residents back once the war ended which eventually did end in five years. However, everyone was brought back except for the twins since the tracker detached from their spaceship causing them to end up on Earth. The parents had no idea where the twins were until they caught frequencies from Earth and tracked the planet down to rescue them.

All of kids' mouths were open. They had no idea what they were hearing. A tear of joy slipped down Myran's cheeks and he gave his father and mother a strangling hug. So did Miffina. Isabella questioned, "So our parents are here too?" Mr and Mrs Feal nodded. The doorbell rang again. All three of them rushed to open the door teeming with joy. A bunch of adults were standing outside with an ear-wide grin. It was a miracle.

Everyone gave their parents a tight hug. After catching up for a while, the parents realised that they had to rush to an event and so exited the house. Rovendy immediately stood up firm and straight and pointed out that everything was not as it seemed. "They could have conveniently faked their identity in order to gather more intel about us. How much do they know about us?" asked Rovendy.

Isabella suggested that they should keep their previous plan on hold and ask Aladana two questions. The first was for information on their parents and the second was to directly confront her about bringing them there. They all shrugged their shoulders, feeling exhausted from the day's work and knowing they had more to do the next day. They were prepared to be shocked once again.

After a long time, they finally felt prepared and ready with a strategy. A sense of relief washed over them as they felt one step closer to the truth. As they settled into their beds, Rovendy asked when they would get to ask all this to Ms. Aladana. Surlay chuckled, suggesting that they could all get detention and meet in the principal's office to talk to her. Myran agreed but also noted the risk involved in Rovendy's plan.

They decided to ask if they could speak to Ms Aladana after lunch the next day, as they believed she would be eager to talk to them, especially after their encounter of the previous day. It seemed like a good plan so they all agreed to go ahead with it. Finally, they turned off the lamps and went to sleep.

CHAPTER SIX

A Shocking Revelation

Everyone was rushing from one end to another as they were running late for the school. Just in time, they left the house, locked it and ran to college. They had a joint session right before lunch which was perfect for them in order to discuss what they had to say to Aladana.

All of them headed off to class. Time flew by fast. Within a few hours, they reached the study hall where all the wings would study and complete pending work. The five found themselves an inconspicuous spot in the corner to discuss the big move they were going to play right after lunch. Miffina suggested, "I say we get right to the point and try to uncover the truth. If she's not involved, she's got nothing to hide."

Miss Danzella, the senior coordinator, came up to the five of them and stared at them intently. It looked like she was glaring, which wasn't a pleasant surprise. She said gruffly, "Miss Aladana would like to have a chat with the five of you in her office right now. So skedaddle. The principal is not a patient woman." All of them exchanged tensed looks. Could it be? Did Aladana know? What was she going to say? Well, they were going to find out.

They all rushed to Miss Aladana's office, giving approving looks to each other - with a tint of tension - and entered the grand doors. They sat on the elongated couch as Miss A - as everyone liked to call her - gestured them to. They all took a deep breath as she started, "Let's cut to the chase. What do you want to ask?"

Before Miffina could start talking, Isabella pleaded with her to answer with full honesty as they needed the information, which could be important to her and the board as well. Miss A nodded. Rovendy then asked if she was aware of the adults who are claiming to be their parents, saying they had barged into their house the previous night. Miss A, looking confused, apologized and told them that their parents had died in a terrible accident. Myran exclaimed that the adults had told them they were given away in a spaceship because of a civil war. Miss A chuckled and informed them that there had been peace for ten centuries. They all raised an eyebrow but Aladana did not react.

Before Miffina could ask her second question, Miss A suggested they put it on hold until they had further sorted out the threat to the safety of the beings on the planet. They all agreed. Miss A then mentioned that since they were still living together, the adults were likely to visit them often. Miffina informed her that they had said they would visit every weekend, which meant in three days. Aladana, thought and decided to come to their house on Saturday and pretend to be a friend they had met on Earth without using her powers. She then hurried them outside the door, as though she had a plan in mind which she had to pen down.

Just before the door closed, Surlay asked a random question about shapeshifting on the planet. Miss A confirmed that shapeshifting was possible and handed him a book with information on people who could shapeshift. She then told them to leave. Surlay quickly opened the book and after a quick glance exclaimed that the whole game had changed. The bell rang and everyone had no choice but to go to their respective classrooms. Eventually the school day came to an end and the five of them assembled in their house where Surlay began to explain everything. to the group.

CHAPTER SEVEN

A Game-Changing Theory

He stated that he had a theory that Aladana was a traitor. There was a reaction of shock from everyone present, with a chorus of criticism filling the room. Surlay then exclaimed, "STOP! JUST LISTEN TO ME!" He then continued in a quieter tone, explaining that he had always found Aladana suspicious. He mentioned that they had tried to question her multiple times without success, and that her sudden rush after learning about their fake parents seemed too coincidental. Additionally, he pointed out that all principals in the college needed a degree in shapeshifting and when he asked Aladana about it, she quickly provided him with a list of shapeshifters. Upon further investigation, he discovered a ripped page in a book, with Aladana's name on the index. He believed that she tore the page to hide her involvement but forgot to remove her name from the index.

The room descended into a profound stillness with each of them consumed by their own thoughts regarding the potential implications of shape-shifting as the key to unlock the mystery at hand. Myran's proposition lingered in the air breeding a sense of discomfort among the group as they grappled with the potential ramifications. This particular scenario had never crossed their minds before, intensifying the tension in the room as they realized the extent of the puzzle that still lay before them. The imminent meeting with the parents now held even greater significance, as they had a fresh perspective to delve into during their pursuit of the truth. The burden of the unknown seemed to weigh heavily on their shoulders, guiding them towards a path that was uncertain and riddled with doubt. An air of anxious anticipation permeated the room as they eagerly awaited the opportunity to put Myran's plan to test.

Everyone noticed how silent Rovendy had been since the start of the conversation. It was pointed out that he seemed to notice that everyone had started staring at him so he cleared his throat and expressed his concern about overreacting to the situation. Isabella pointed out that they couldn't rely on a "what if," as they could be in serious trouble if they were wrong but the consequences could be even worse if they were right. She reassured Rovendy that they wouldn't proceed with any plan until everyone in the room agreed, emphasizing the importance of unity. Rovendy appeared relieved and nodded slowly indicating his agreement. They all decided to end the discussion early as they were all mentally drained. The next day held the potential to be pivotal that could alter their fate and the fate of the world.

They all woke up to the sight of grey fluffy clouds shrouding the sun as the air became moist heralding the beginning of a terrible storm. It looked as if the weather was not on their side at all. It didn't uplift their spirits.

After freshening up, they all gathered around the table for breakfast. Miffina questioned, "Is everyone ready?" They all nodded. They finished eating their meals and relaxed in the lounge. That was rather one good thing about weekends. There was no school and so eventually their stress level, which was sky-rocketing recently would hopefully plummet.

Myran sadly acknowledged that this weekend was going to be full of unpleasant events. As the door rang in unison with the rumbling of the clouds, he took a deep breath before opening it to find Miss A and all the other parents standing outside. Miss A laughed and informed him that there was a misunderstanding with his parents but assured him that he need not concern himself with the details. Gesturing them to come inside, Myran looked puzzled as Surlay asked about the whereabouts of his mother. His father explained that she was not feeling well and had decided to stay home and rest. Isabella pointed out the resemblance between Miss A and Surlay's mom, causing Miss Aladana to try to avoid her gaze. Sensing this, Isabella questioned if she had done something wrong and mentioned the similarity in their voices, comparing them to characters from "Downton Abbey." Miss A's temper began to rise at the comparison.

Miss Aladana shrieked, "Enough! I have had enough from you Miss Fonx. What are you suggesting I am Surlay's mother?" Isabella flashed a smirk and replied, "Partially yes. But rather I'm trying to stress the fact that you are going through quite some limits to try to be disguised. You've given away yourself a little too much. See this?" She grabbed the book of Shapeshifters. "Where is your name? Oh right, you tore that exact page number. I think I have enough evidence to prove your guilt. Wouldn't it be so much easier for you to admit so that we don't have to play this little game? It truly flusters me." Aladana forcedly sighed and said sarcastically, "Fine you caught me. Congratulations! I-" Surlay interrupted saying, "Right we will be doing the talking. Your reply to what you are asked. First off, why be in disguise? What are you up to? Why did you bring us here?"

Miss A expressed that they wanted the five to approach the information with an open mind and acknowledged that it might be intense. She began by saying that Earth was once a planet full of life and described a perfect society where there were no crimes, no injustice, and unfair events. Everything fell apart in less than thirty minutes due to the actions of one person, Sachel Salegio, who attempted to create a separate species. She revealed that humans were the result of Sachel's failed experiment and described humans as beings capable of manipulation, destruction, and despair. Aladana and her friends had discussed a plan to reclaim their home planet from humans, whom they deemed unworthy of existence. She mentioned that the five had been brought home to prevent them from being influenced by humans and hoped that they would join forces in the fight against humans. Miss Aladana considered that disguises were necessary to avoid controversy and protests. She concluded by stating that they were truly their parents and expressed their belief that the kids would support their cause.

Myran scoffed. He pointed out that it could be a lie again. Who was to be sure? However, the others shared a mutual understanding and they believed that they weren't lying because their identities were revealed. There was nothing to hide. Nevertheless, they were all enraged by their parent's ideas. It was believable that they were crumpled down and forced into the fringes but causing a whole human apocalypse? They couldn't let that happen. They had to convince their parents that humans had changed over time. Yes, they were still pretty selfish but not everyone turned on the other. They had to think of a solid argument to support their opinion. They needed a plan and had to improvise on the spot.

Before they could start, Miffina strode towards their parent's side and said, "After hearing the story, I believe that humans don't deserve to exist. We've only seen the upper layer of them but deep down they will always be backstabbing traitors." Isabella stared in absolute disbelief. "Miffina, this isn't you. You loved humans. You-" Miffina said savagely, "Stop living in the past." Myran went over to his sister, held her hand and said, "Miffy, we have always been together, you can't leave me now" Everyone could see the pain in Miffina's eyes. They were welling up. However, she forcefully let go of Myran's hand and said, "Let's go Miss A. I am not going to be with a bunch of human lovers." Miss A chuckled with satisfaction, held Miffina's hand and everyone except the remaining four went. They were heartbroken. They considered Miffina to be the most loyal out of them all. Her betrayal hit everyone immensely.

Everyone put their hand on Myran's shoulder. They couldn't even imagine how hard it must have been for him. The Mylia Twins used to do everything together. Later that night they tried falling asleep but ,as expected, no one was able to. However, they all knew one thing- nothing would ever be the same.

CHAPTER EIGHT

THE BOARD OF MYSAINS

The sun decided to rest in slumber for a prolonged period than it was supposed to. They all woke up to a night sky at seven in the morning. The aura of the house didn't change. The sorrow, disgust, hatred and confusion of Miffina's betrayal lingered. The world didn't seem real anymore. They all freshened up - except Myran - and sat on the table for the morning coffee. Miffina would usually make the coffee. However, due to the circumstances, Isabella made it. All of them released a small chuckle.

Rovendy spoke softly, "At least we found one thing about Isabella: she isn't good at cooking." Isabella couldn't even manage to laugh silently. Everyone was wondering the whereabouts of Myran. However, they concluded that he needed some space after the dramatic incident that had taken place.

A few hours passed. The three of them continued talking about what all they had left for homework from school, for they were swarmed with it and not much time was left to complete it especially with all the things that were going on. All of a sudden, Myran appeared with his hair dishevelled. His eyes were swollen and he was full of bruises. All of them rushed towards him. Surlay bought the first-aid kit while Isabella attended to his wounds. She looked in complete shock and asked, "Did you get into a fight?" Rovendy motioned Isabella to move and asked in his surprisingly soothing voice, "Tell us what happened."

Myran started explaining, " I was in denial that Miffina would betray us. So, I snuck out of the house at night in search of her. I found her on the street in front with bodyguards. I tried approaching her but the bodyguards stayed still and blocked my path. I tried to explain to them that I just wanted to talk but they attacked me. I took down three but the last one hit me hard. The worst part was that I could not see a quiver of guilt nor tears in Miffina's eyes."

He was bleeding and crying profusely. After a few minutes, Isabella managed to stop excessive blood loss and healed his wounds temporarily. In the meanwhile, both the boys tried calming Myran down. Surlay said inspiringly, "The road to success is never a straight line. There are mountains, hills and valleys but we don't give up or lose hope. We have had a sharp fall. But we need to convert that negativity to positivity and rise to the occasion." They all nodded.

They were all thinking about their next move. Whatever it was, they had to do it fast, for a whole species depended on it. Rovendy suggested that they persuade the Board Of Mysains to withdraw their decision by personally talking to them. It seemed like the best option on the table so they decided that they would go ahead with it.

All they had to do was set up a meeting with the Board. That was going to be a real task. The only person they knew who could set up a meeting, was Miss A, who would not support them in this decision. They had to find someone.

Someone who had good relations with the Board because they needed a good impression to even have a chance of success.

Miss Aladana had a good relation with the board. She helped plant the idea of the destruction of Earth which the Board wanted to get done. In addition, they didn't know anyone else who could help them. Isabella thought of lying to Miss A, in order to get her to agree. The real issue had to be between the Board and them. Moreover, she was sure that the Board would at least value their want for discretion upon the matter. It was decided and final.

As the noon approached, the heat scorched the bare land. It was a burning hot Sunday. Despite the weather conditions - being in triple-digit figures - they had to go to school and book an appointment with Miss Aladana, who they could hopefully convince to book an appointment with The Board Of Mysains. They all got dressed in their best formal outfits, took a hover taxi and arrived at the school. They walked over to the receptionist and requested an appointment with Miss A.

Aladana had a long line of meetings, so they had to wait for at least an hour. Isabella put on her death stare, and said savagely, "Tell her our names, and I'm positive she will squeeze us in." The receptionist gulped and asked for their names. Isabella told all four of their names and the receptionist - who Isabella recognised to be Miss Danzella - called Miss A. The four of them were called immediately to her office. As much as they hated Miss Aladana, they had to act nice and go with the flow to at least have a forlorn chance of meeting the board.

They all had to climb the miserably long staircases. After more than thirty minutes, they reached Miss Aladana's office. They knocked at the door and without any affirmation from the principal, they walked inside and fell on the sofa, feeling fifty pounds heavier. Miss Aladana said mockingly, "I hope your journey was enjoyable. The steps are quite necessary because most kids come to my office as they have caused some trouble. Their remorse must be so much by climbing the steps, that they beg for my mercy. Works like a charm. Proceed with what you have to say."

Rovendy decided to take the lead on this. He started, "We believe that you can set up a meeting with the council." She nodded. "Would you be interested in doing the same for us?" Miss A scratched her chin, and said, "I would be glad to. I'll just check when the Board is free for a meeting." Surprised, they talked no more to make sure that they don't light a bomb nor change her mind.

All four of them looked down. She had a valid point-one they didn't think of. But it was their only option. They agreed for the meeting. While Aladana was calling the Board, the four of them slouched on the couch with their legs splayed. A few awkward moments flew by. Miss Aladana finally spoke after a very long conversation with the Board, "They have agreed to talk to you. Warning, you might want to rush. They want to meet you in an hour starting now. Grab a taxi after you get changed and go to the Sementrem Slackery. Over there go to the lobby and tell them about your appointment and they'll let you in. Toodles now." The four of them immediately got up, sprinted down the staircases and dashed to their house. They got changed into semi-formal clothes. They took a minute in stealing the mirror from each other to see how they were looking and rushed downstairs.

They stood still. They couldn't see anything in the traffic that lay ahead of them. All the honking made them feel slightly dizzy. After a few minutes, they found a hover taxi. They jumped in and informed the driver about their destination. The traffic started moving. While driving, the driver inquired, "Are you going to meet to the board?" They replied in awe, "Yes we are. How did you know?" He said, "Most people always go to Sementrem Slackery to meet the Board. Rather, it's the only reason. There is nothing else to do over there apart from gazing upon the lame achievements of the Board." Surlay snorted. Rovendy asked, "Do people here like the Board Of Mysains?" He replied, "Partially , however; it is not our choice to make. The Board is decided by bloodline. People have been begging for a voting system but they have not been in favour of such a thing. I hear on Earth there is." They nodded. "It's called democracy," Isabella said. Within thirty minutes, they reached Sementrem Slackery. They got off, thanked and paid the driver and started walking towards their destination.

The Sementrem Slackery was surely a grand building as expected. The rooftop was supported by intricate pillars while an abundance of greenery was present. There were huge polished wooden doors at the entrance. The area in which this place was situated looked like a pretty European town. They entered the grand hall. The paintings were classic Roman, with a crystal clear marble floor. They hurried to the reception and told her that they had a meeting with the Board. They entered their names and were granted entry. They were told that the Board was sitting in room Three, on the top floor. Luckily there was a lift, so they entered the lift and reached the respective floor. They walked through the endless corridors and finally found Room Three. They knocked at the door and waited. After a few minutes, a deep voice announced, "Come in."

Anxiously, they opened the door. The room was not as fancy as they were expecting. It was mediocre-sized, with one bright tube light illuminating the whole room. There were six councillors, with their names on each of their desks. Councillor Aliea asked, "We hope you have something serious to discuss. We had a meeting but cancelled it because Aladana called and said you wanted to say something. We agreed because you are still new in our world." Isabella decided to take the lead on this, "Your Board eminences, we would first like a confirmation that whatever discussion happens here, stays within this room." All six of them nodded. She continued, "We have attained information of your approval for the invasion and eradication of planet Earth due to your formidable past. We have come to deliberate over this topic." Councillor Elengton said in outrage, "How do you know this? Who told you? I will smash them into a pit of darkness!" Isabella said confidently, "We coaxed the information out of Miss Aladana and our parents. Anyways, this is going off-topic." Even Councillors Windsor, Ilaria, Catronia and Mateo were still steaming mad. It was time for Rovendy to step in with his soothing voice.

"Excuse me councillors. This meeting was for discussion purposes only. We would certainly respect a dignified and fruitful discussion from both sides." All the councillors immediately stopped their blabbering. Councillor Windsor - who turned out to be the leader - said, "Our sincere apologies. You are right. Go on." Surlay continued, "We do not side with this decision of yours. Once humans in the past did horrendous things. But they have changed over time. Barely anyone is bad now." All the councillors were whispering. They all waited anxiously. After a few moments, Councillor Ilaria said, "After much discussion we believe that we should". Ilaria continued, "Declare war on the humans!" All of their joy faded away. They were shocked to hear this especially after that amazing speech they gave. Their happiness had a very short life which faded away instantly. Isabella shot mocking remarks at all the councillors. The three boys dragged her out of the room. All of them walked through the hallway, downcast. They all shared one thought.

They had to stop this, no matter what, when, or who would stand in their way.

CHAPTER NINE

THE TRUTH

"Did it go well?" asked the taxi driver. They all stayed silent and hopped in the vehicle. He understood immediately. He tried his best to console them and they appreciated it, however; they were racking their heads hard trying to think of a plan. After a few minutes, a red light came and they were presented with an abrupt halt. The driver said, "I suppose it is time I should hand you this." He gave them a chit of paper with a printed message.

*"A person in disguise is the one you must find. For the criminals are always the least suspected of them all. When your brain says no, know that your heart will not concur, and to your lead suspect shall you be brought. ---- **Sachel Salegio**"*

They all stared at the chit that was handed over to them. The taxi driver mentioned that Sachel and him were good friends and she had given him this note right before disappearing into thin air. She had told him to pass it on to the people who could save their world from impending doom. They all were confounded. After a few hours, they reached their house. They thanked the driver, paid him generously and fell on the sofas. All of them were immensely tired so they decided to take a short nap to replenish their significantly dwindling energy.

After a few hours, they came into the living room and sat at the dining table. No one was ready to talk about what happened. It was a disappointing day. Something struck Rovendy. He grabbed his Fineomatic history textbook, as he frantically skimmed through the pages looking for a certain page. After a while, he found it. It was mentioned that legend had it that Sachel had passed a note to a mysterious person right before her disappearance. No-one knew what was written on it. All of them gasped.

Surlay took the chit and discovered a number at the back of it. He dialled it on the telephone. It was the driver. Surlay confronted the taxi driver telling him that they knew who he was, and that they needed to talk. They asked him to pick them up at ten a.m. sharp.

Just as Myran was going back to the couch, the telephone started ringing again. Isabella raised an eyebrow and picked up in an agitated mood, as they had just talked. "What?" she scowled angrily. A deep voice answered. They were told that it was Sachel. She informed that she wasn't available at ten, so she would meet them at six. The line was then cut.

By the time they were ready to leave, it was already quarter to six. They rushed down to the main gate and waited apprehensively. In the flash of an eye, a peculiar-looking vehicle teleported out of the blue. Inside the car was Miss Danzella. She stepped out of the car and declared, "There were a few changes in the plan. Sachel sent me instead. Now hop in the car. I believe she mentioned that you couldn't afford to be late." Gulping, they hopped in the car. She pressed the accelerator hard, as they were pushed back into their seats. Soon enough, the whole city disappeared from eyesight.

Something was off. Danzella sensed the awkward silence and started, "I have been keeping an eye on you ever since you left our planet. However, when you were brought back, it was sadly harder. With so many people on the Board keeping track of you, I couldn't risk getting caught. So I decided to keep watching you physically. I knew Aladana and her friends had planned on destroying Earth from before. They were just waiting for your return. The whole world is in chaos right now, which I can take advantage of. I see this as an opportunity to rise and get the respect I deserve."

They all burst into laughter. Danzella felt offended. Myran pointed out, "You and what army can take over this planet? What makes you think Earth will back down?" Miss Danzella felt agitated enough and said, "My robot army and all of you." Myran seemed bemused. While all of them would never side with Danzella, they all knew that she was a powerful woman and was capable of just about anything. If she was making a mountain of a claim, they had to take it seriously.

Pretending not to hear the last statement , Rovendy asked, "How did you manage to be at so many places and be so many people?" She scoffed, "I killed them and covered up their death and no one even noticed." They all found that impossible. One death cover-up, still possible. But three? There was something wrong. They felt as if Miss Danzella was in their head when she said, "I use a chip which I call Der Zertrümmerer. It makes a victim go somewhere forbidden, causing their death. It also uses DNA connections to make people who know the victim forget about their relationship with them."

CHAPTER TEN

ENEMIES

After a long period of silence, Danzella asked the four of them to drink some special water as she handed the cups to them. All of them were about to take a sip when Myran smartly stopped them. He pointed out that they couldn't trust her in anything, considering what she had done or was going to do. Miss Danzella put their suspicion to rest by drinking a sip of the water that was kept next to her.

Everyone still seemed unconvinced, except Rovendy. In order to quench his unbearable thirst, he took a sip of the water. After a few seconds, he shrugged his shoulders. Everything seemed okay at that moment.

Right before the others were going to drink, Rovendy started vibrating like a building suffering from an earthquake. Smoke came out from his eyes and then he lay flat on the floor. They all stared at his unconscious body. Isabella looked savagely into the eyes of Miss Danzella. Just a few moments before she was about to pounce, Surlay stopped her and pointed at Rovendy, who was now floating in mid-air. His eyes turned pure purple.

He flew to Miss Danzella and bowed in front of her. The three of them put their hands on their mouths. Miss Danzella gave an ear-wide grin. Suddenly, she took an abrupt turn and took all of them back to their house. The three of them got off. They consistently asked Rovendy to get down but he refused every time. She said brutally, "He's mine now!" and flew off like the wind.

Surlay growled and stormed inside the house. Isabella and Myran followed him inside. He fell on the chair, his back slouched and started sobbing. Myran hugged him, while Isabella stood on the side with a vexed yet thoughtful expression. Most people would have expected her to go raging mad or show immense frustration. Instead, she flashed a smile on her face. Both of them raised an eyebrow.

She declared, " I'm amused. Think about it: all our parents aimed to break our group to get more people. Danzella wanted to get us on her side and Sachel agreed to the meeting, which is quite peculiar given her circumstances. It was a trap. Our enemies are afraid of us. We need to retaliate and strike on their weak spots."

They all wanted to plan some schemes, but were too tired to. So, they decided to do it as the first thing the next morning. They had enough on their plate to think about. They were going to hit all three of their enemies hard and shatter them on the next day. They each took an enemy in mind to work on. They all had some food and went into their rooms. They were all fast asleep before nightfall arrived.

All of them got up much before dawn to plan and assembled at the table to discuss their ideas at eight. As usual, Isabella made tea and coffee, while both the boys set the table and all the three blueprints they had made. Myran requested to start. They all agreed.

He started by saying that there were two parts to his plan. They had to get Miffina back to their side and take down Aladana. The only reason Miffina was with Miss A was because she believed that Earth betrayed them. With the right amount of persuasion they could get her back. The only problem was that the last time Myran tried approaching her, he came back swollen like a tomato. So, they had to pay Miffina a visit in school, where she would be attending the lectures without bodyguards.

He stated that there were two parts to his plan, which involved rescuing Miffina and dismantling the organization. He believed that Miffina would likely be involved with the group due to the fact that they had a semi valid reason to do so. He thought the best approach to retrieve her without violence was to expose flaws in their scheme, causing her to doubt its success. Both Isabella and Surlay were impressed by his strategy. Isabella inquired about the specific weaknesses he had identified. He explained that the group leaders, including Miss A and their parents, lacked understanding of human nature on Earth and underestimated the potential backlash. He predicted that Earth would mobilize its advanced weaponry, including ballistic missiles and nuclear bombs in defence. He highlighted the united willpower of the Earth's citizens, suggesting that even rival nations like Russia and the US would collaborate. Myran acknowledged that Miffina required concrete evidence to be persuaded, as she valued facts and statistics. Isabella agreed, and Myran asserted his unique understanding of his sister's mindset as her brother. Isabella suggested revisiting the rescue plan later, to which Myran reluctantly agreed.

They discussed the need to first locate Miss A and their parents' coordinates. Myran suggested breaking into Miss A's office to gather information. Later that day, they could visit Miss A's office after school, as they had heard she never leaves and even sleeps there. He had overheard Miss

A scheduling a meeting for four p.m. and decided to confirm if she would be free at that time. He also mentioned finding some gadgets in Miss A's office, which they believed could bypass security measures. They planned to break in, restrain Miss A, gather information and potentially threaten her. Isabella decided to target Danzella next.

She started explaining that she felt it was pretty easy to take down Danzella, with the only problem being that they didn't have a fair idea about Miss Danzella compared to their other enemies. She proceeded to outline her plan, mentioning that Miss Danzella could be in three different places the next day - the reception of Sementrem Slackery, at the university, or with Sachel. She mentioned that she had to go to the university for a project submission and asked if the others had anything necessary there as well. They both shook their heads, so she assigned Surlay to check with Sachel and Myran to go to the Sementrem Slackery. She assured them that she would make excuses for their absences and that they would be each other's backup.

Surlay interrupted, questioning why they were discussing the plan for the next day when the timings were overlapping and in what order everything would happen. Isabella explained that she had planned for the whole week and needed them to hear her out completely. She went on to explain their plan to rescue Rovendy, mentioning that he had exams the following week which included a spell that could counter Danzella's. She planned to mix the counter spell into Rovendy's food during lunch.

Lastly, Isabella mentioned the plan to take down Danzella, stating that once someone found her, they should call everyone else to the location so they could all take her down together. She emphasized the importance of waiting for a signal after Rovendy was rescued before revealing Danzella's location. She warned that the plan could go awry if not followed correctly.

Myran announced that Miss Danzella was talking about a robot army in her defence. Isabella replied smartly that the robots take time to be assembled and Danzella was saving them for her big move. She also mentioned that Danzella believed she was giving away her true intensions. Isabella explained that Danzella didn't want the matter to go to the board as they would have conducted investigations, giving her no time to escape. Isabella emphasized the need for solid evidence to prove Danzella's guilt, knowing that the Board would take time to look into it. Isabella also mentioned that Danzella, being the receptionist, knows the Board's schedule and can use that time to investigate. Isabella warned Surlay to be on alert as Danzella might be with Sachel if not in school, using her robots discreetly to avoid attracting attention. The two of them found the plan to be solid.

Myran inquired if Surlay had any information, noting that the blueprint only showed a human outline with a silhouette. Surlay replied by expressing uncertainty about Sachel's allegiance and questioning why Sachel would agree to meet with them after being in hiding for so long. Surlay emphasized the importance of determining Sachel's involvement with Danzella and suggested setting up a private meeting to gather information. Surlay acknowledged the challenges in persuading Sachel to cooperate, considering their lack of knowledge about her intentions. The possibility of Sachel being allied with Danzella was also raised as a potential threat. Surlay highlighted the urgency of meeting with Sachel before taking any further actions.

They discussed and decided that Isabella's and Surlay's plans could be executed on the same day, for he could also interrogate Sachel. If they were lucky, and Sachel didn't know about Danzella, it would work to their advantage. Sachel herself would throw out Danzella and would come on their side. However, they didn't want to count their chickens before they hatched. They concluded to go with Myran's plan the next day; Isabella's and Surlay's the day after.

CHAPTER ELEVEN

A Slice Of The Pie

The day began high-spirited. They all sprang out of bed; packed their bags and gadgets; changed and rushed off to school. It turned out that they were a little early for school, and so the gates were closed. All they could do was wait. After a few minutes - that felt like hours - the school gates opened; however, no one was there.

There were no staff, students, helpers. They started walking down the now eerie hallways looking around if they could find anyone. Surlay saw the time and told them that they were on time. All the lights were also off. All of a sudden, a dark shadow appeared. Slowly, the person emerged in the light and became instantly recognisable. The white dyed curly hair, the wrapped purple gown, the snake-like outline on the dress, along with the bright red lipstick was surely Miss Aladana. Right behind her were their parents and Miffina.

Myran slowly pulled out his phone and started recording. He made sure that he was discreet enough to ensure that he wasn't easily noticed recording.

Miss Aladana said maliciously, "We had emailed everyone that the school would remain closed today, except for you. We supposed this was going to come because the teacher that you called Myran, confirmed with me. You got to know I never leave the office. You must have thought it would be the perfect opportunity to take us down. It was all the matter to get inside your head."

The three of them couldn't believe it. Something, however, struck Isabella. If they were thinking so much, why hadn't they pointed out that Rovendy wasn't there with them? They couldn't have forgotten. Miss A and her team knew more than they were letting on. She beckoned both the boys and allured them to go back to their house.

Aladana said with a smirk, "Danzella is working with us. She will help us cripple the Board. We can't afford the Board Of Mysains to know about our ulterior motives. You know too much. We must destroy you before you reveal that tape you are holding Myran. I-" In the blink of an eye, all of them used the teleportation device and reached their house.

The powerful device created a tremendous blow when they reached the house. They fell flat on the wooden floor. After a few minutes, they all stood up and fell on the sofa. Isabella explained her observations to them. They found them valid. It occurred to them that Danzella must have been getting everyone to do parts of her plan, without them knowing: small pieces of the pie, but no one except her knew the whole thing.

They had to uncover Danzella's plot before she could employ it. Danzella's main motive was to get both planets destroyed. She must have been in contact with Aladana and tricked her into thinking she was only on her side. Currently, Aladana believed that Danzella was only with her. That way, Miss Danzella got half of her work done. The only question was, how was she planning to get their homeland killed? Could Sachel have been involved in this? They had to set up a meeting as soon as possible.

Surlay got up and headed towards the telephone. He went through the list of numbers that were engaged in a conversation. Within a few seconds, he had found it. He quickly dialled the number on the telephone. It was ringing. "Hello? Who is this?" asked Sachel on the other side. "Surlay speaking. Our last meeting got cancelled due to some emergency, so we forgot to inform you. We would like to meet up this time. As soon as possible, for the matter is quite urgent and possibly delicate." She replied, "Tomorrow five o'clock. Don't be late." The line got cut.

He nodded to Isabella and Myran, as they did back. They had secrets to uncover and mysteries to solve. When they first arrived, all they could think about was whether they would pass their exam or not. Now, they had bigger fish to fry. The race of the two species rested like a burden on their shoulder as they were given huge responsibilities unknowingly.

CHAPTER TWELVE

PERSPECTIVE

"Hurry! We need to leave," shouted Myran. Isabella and Rovendy frantically rushed downstairs as they wore their jackets. All three of them wore their shoes and rushed out of the house. They were expecting someone to come and pick them up, like last time. Well, that wasn't ideal. Isabella took out her phone and rang Sachel. She was told that the address of her location was her number.

All three of them looked at the number. It was a ten-digit number. Rovendy exclaimed, "I got it! These numbers must signify street numbers, road junctions, the number of the building and house number." Myran patted his back, complimenting him with a glint of sarcasm in his voice. They were on Street Twelve and had to get to Street Nine. They asked a few people and made it there. Second, the road number. They were on the right road. They went building to building and after some moments flew by, they found the building. It looked more like a three-story house. They all took a deep breath and rang the doorbell.

It seemed to be unlocked so they pushed the door open. It opened with a creek as it brought in view the eerie hallway they were going to pass. Holding each other's hand, they stepped in bravely. They walked along the single path made of broken wood and plain cement. After more than five hundred steps, they came to the end of the hallway and were presented with a door made of dark polished wood.

Slowly, they turned the door knob and pushed against it gently. However, it did not open. They tried with more force each time but it did not open. No matter what they tried it did not budge. Surlay fell on the floor and tears started flowing down his cheeks. Isabella questioned, "Surlay, what happened? Why are you getting so emotional?" He replied, "Oh, it's not sad tears. I feel like someone is boiling onions. It's searing my eyes." She raised an eyebrow, as did Myran. Both of them could not feel anything. However, Myran pointed out the fact that Surlay had hyper-aware senses so he would get affected by the slightest change in the environment, which was strange, given his thundomatic abilities.

Next moment, a doorbell appeared on the side of the wall. Isabella rang it. Immediately, the door opened. All three of them stepped in and found themselves surrounded by grey bricks and many concrete shelves. The room was lit by a bright, single turquoise light coming from underneath one of the shelves. The hearth was brought to life by a crackling fire while green plants shrouded the sink made of an alloy. Right through the wall, came an elderly-looking woman. Her hairs were thin like strings and looked as if they were painted white. Her skin was all wrinkled and white like a ghost. Surlay asked, "Are you Sachel?" She replied, "Yes, I-" She was interrupted by a deep voice, "Am not. I am Sachel. So, we have loads to talk about, or should I say, you do. Follow me." They nodded.

Sachel's hair was tied in a tight ponytail, moving side to side as she walked while her elegant purple gown swept the floor like a mop. She opened a door outlined with beautiful glowing rocks. She led them inside her lounge area, with big red sofas and a massive glass table. The yellow light contributed to the surprisingly serene ambience. They all pictured Sachel living in a house in ramshackle, or at least for her to have an eccentric personality as they watched in movies back on Earth. They took a seat on the couch, while Sachel gave them some water. Before even taking a sip, Isabella asked, "Is this-" She was interrupted again by Sachel, "Yes, this is pure water. I recall an incident of Danzella using the manipulative water to get Rovendy. Well, let me assure you that I am on your side. We have time to talk about it. But first, would you like some tea?" They nodded, still surprised by Sachel's answer. She smiled, got up, and went to the kitchen.

Isabella asked Sachel why she had agreed to meet with a random group of teenagers who were likely of no use to her after they all exchanged looks and sat in silence until Sachel arrived with hot tea, warning them to be careful. Sachel explained that she had sent Danzella to pick them up, but when she called Danzella after she had been gone for a while, she overheard a conversation that made her realize Danzella was not being careful. Sachel then told Danzella to not bother coming back, and they both shared a mutual agreement.

Sachel announced that they were her creations. They all stared at her in suspense and confusion. She explained that she had realized her earlier experiment had gone wrong and had tried to make a rectified version, which had worked. However, before it could stop her original creation - Wrangler - it was injured by people on Earth who thought it was a mistake like Wrangler. The descendants of Wrangler were a better version. Sachel believed things had changed on Earth over time, but their people never forgot the past and were stuck. Rovendy had asked Sachel why she referred to them and the other people on their planet as 'your people' and not 'our people.' She had replied that she would never align herself with such merciless people, a sentiment they found quite valid.

They were still thinking about whether to trust Sachel or not. By all standards, the story seemed quite possible but they didn't know her. How could they have known whether she was telling a lie right then? The three of them were in such a position that they didn't know whom to trust. One wrong move could be fatal. "Why should we trust you?" Isabella asked. Sachel replied with a smirk, "I don't care whether you do or not. I don't lose anything with or without you. That's your choice to make. I don't need anything to prove myself. For all you know, I could be Aladana pretending to be Sachel." They all gave her a look screaming: Who's side are you on? She immediately caught that on. All Sachel did was shrug her shoulders.

They all agreed that Sachel was not Aladana, for she would pull whoever she could onto her side. They also felt that Sachel would be a great asset to them, for she had common sense and seemed quite reasonable as far as they observed. However, one thing that was impeding from getting her to their side was her attitude. Sachel seemed too casual with what she was doing. It was a high possibility that she could easily leak out their plan. They had to be careful with her.

Isabella reached out her hand for a handshake. Sachel lifted her hand the same way. The three of them welcomed her into the team. Sachel explained, "We might need to have make attending these meetings a habit. Take these phones. They have a secure line. I'll change places for every meeting. I'll ping you the location the same way I did today." She handed them the small phones and politely but forcefully made them leave her house.

Feeling slightly happy after a long time, they took a taxi and reached their house. They all went to Myran's bedroom, for they were too exhausted to tidy up the house. They all shared a mutual understanding that things would get better since they had gotten Sachel on their side. Myran said wisely, "Perspective! That's how we beat our enemies. The only way Aladana knew we would come was because she saw things from our perspective. Till now, we anticipated our enemies' moves by thinking about what would be the logical move. If we want to get into our enemies' heads, we have to think like them." Isabella's and Rovendy's eyeballs stuck out wide open. That was something they had surprisingly never thought of. Right after that, something struck them.

The lady in the kitchen at Sachel's house seemed suspicious. She tried to say that she was Sachel. Right after that, the real Sachel came. Why would she try to impersonate Sachel? Knowing Aladana, she would always take such opportunities. She would try to get people on her side. They had to keep a close eye on her. Danzella could have conveyed the message to Aladana to shapeshift into the helper. Something fishy was going on, and they had to find out.

CHAPTER THIRTEEN

THE REVELATION

In a battle with many players, focusing on the wrong one could be fatal. That was the last line Aladana said to the three of them in their previous visit. She hinted at something important which they had to find out. They called Sachel to inform her about their plan. She thought it was fine but warned them to be careful. Sachel told them to meet her at the location she had just sent them before school started on the telephone. She sent them a ten-digit number. They nodded to each other and went to their respective beds to sleep, for they had to get up early the next day before the university started. Time went by in the snap of a finger. Before they knew it, the Sun's rays appeared right above the beautiful dusky-orange horizon. They jumped out of the bed, did all their morning chores, changed and headed towards the coordinates. They entered the doors of what happened to be an extravagant five-star hotel. Entering the lift, they clicked the button and made their way across the long hallway. They knocked at the door. In less than a second, the door opened. Sachel opened it, her hair beyond tousled. She gestured them to come in.

"I was up, running scenarios for what Aladana might have in store. There is a possibility that Aladana might have sent a little message to all the students again that the university wouldn't be working today. I had to be double-sure, so I tried hacking into Aladana's Google account. She has a lot of security, which took hours of coding to get by. Either way, I got into it - attracting no suspicion - and tried going through her laptop for any planner she might have. I found a locked note on her laptop. Got the note right. Found a few days ahead of her plans. Moreover, she has sent everyone except you guys about today's cancellation. So, this time we are a few steps ahead. We should use it wisely. Though there was one thing I was not able to decrypt. Below this in her notes, there are a bunch of weird signs. In all my years, I haven't come across anything like this. It might be important. It has six symbols." She drew the signs and gave them. #!()^$%. It was quite odd. She continued, "They will most probably be waiting for you guys. I only had time to get this done."

The three of them thanked her. They told her that they could take it from there. All of them were struck with the same idea. They requested Sachel to send a message to all the students from Miss A's account that the university would be working that day. However, the timings would be ten-fifteen minutes late and that everyone had to be there on time. Once they see the three of them, they have to wait for a signal and then come. They had to get teleportation devices. Everybody had at least one. They must use the monitors with the password given and see the camera for the signal. The signal would be waving Hi. Miss Aladana would have thought that she would win until she would accidentally spill her secrets. Students would have their phones out, with enough proof to the Board Of Directors. That would be one enemy down.

Right after Sachel performed all the actions, they quickly headed off to the university. By the time they reached, Aladana was already standing right in the middle of the school hallway. The three of them entered. Aladana started, "So you fell for my trap again. Looks like-" Isabella waved her hand. Within seconds, hundreds of students teleported in. "We and Danzella can take over Earth and the Board of Mysains" She stared at the huge crowd of students with their phones up. She screamed in horror. All the students were opened mouthed. All three of them patted each other's back. Myran questioned, "How did you know?" Isabella responded by saying that it was perspective. They knew that Aladana would call them once again to tell them a key point in their plan, thus revealing her and her cronies' intentions. They just had to get inside her head and think like her.

CHAPTER FOURTEEN

SLAYER OF DEMONS

Myran announced, "See everyone? Our president of the university; The most trustworthy member is a traitor. A traitor to us, to our past, and to the rulers of this world." They all nodded their heads, filled with anger. Aladana went mad with laughter, almost collapsing to the floor in a writhing position. She quickly regained her composure, got up and raised both of her hands.

Black, ink-like liquid squirted out of her palm. Black-like creatures formed. Third-semester students whispered worriedly about the creatures being demons. Until the third semester, no one in the university was aware of demons. Miss A seemed quite surprised as she mentioned that she thought that it was added by the first year. "For all those who don't know who demons are :they are creatures of darkness. They suck and drain the happiness from living creatures, eradicate people, they can shapeshift, and a few can manipulate. In this case, however - with months of research - Miss Danzella and I have created demons with our abilities and much more." She beckoned Miffina who was standing unnoticed behind her.

Miffina stepped in front and looked nothing like how they last saw her. Her eyes were like an enlarged black pupil covering her whole eyeball. She motioned some hand gestures towards the demons. They nodded and started chasing all the students. Isabella ordered all of them to stay grounded if they were truly loyal to the university and they did as said. All of the demons stopped abruptly.

All of a sudden they all submerged into the ground and emerged on the opposite side of the ground engaging in a fight with the students. Each of them used their powers. The mass of the demons kept on increasing, so they couldn't just keep erasing demons one at a time. They had to merge. All of them were able to classify the demons into five different groups.

Teleportation, Manipulation, Hardcore Strength, Spells, and Shapeshifters. Now was the time to apply all the practical experiments and theoretical knowledge they did in school to reality. Fortunately for them, the university had taught them to unlock many secrets with their powers. The Dark People would go for the Shapeshifters, for they could identify where they would be.

Hyndofines would go for Teleportation because they could impede the path of the teleporters. The Light People would go for the Manipulative People, due to their ability to create a mental block around their mind. Lightnos would attack Hardcore Strength, while Fineomines would go for Spells.

Aladana said, mildly impressed, "Looks like you all have been paying attention to what has been taught to you. As a reward, we will go systematically. My group of Demons, versus your group of people. Whoever wins the most matches wins. I suppose you must have already divided?" They nodded. Miffina motioned for the first set of demons to come. They tried identifying the batch. They were shapeshifters. All the Dark People stepped up. In the flash of an eye, all the demons disappeared.

While all the Dark People were searching for the shapeshifters, Miffina was busy smirking. Isabella requested Aladana to get Hyndofines to go last. She nodded. Isabella didn't know how much she could trust Miss Aladana, so she had to do it fast.

Isabella flew up in the air. As she hoped, Miffina followed. She stopped mid-air. She found a switch in Miffina's back. As quick as a cheetah, she unplugged it. Miffina started taking abrupt breaths. "Isabella?" Miffina asked groggily. With tears of joy, Isabella gave her a tight hug. Miffina apologised for going there, saying she was confused. Isabella explained to her the whole thing and kept her up to date. They immediately formulated a plan.

Miffina returned to Aladana. She told her that Isabella was dead. Miss A seemed more than pleased. Isabella had already informed the other Hyndofines about her plan. The Dark People were still in the battle with the shapeshifters. If they were going to win, they had to win smartly. Aladana and her team had more people compared to theirs, but they had more brains than them. If they had to win, they couldn't go systematically. It would work to Aladana's advantage. That would explain why she would suggest such an idea out of all people. They had to attack all at once.

Isabella flew in, signalled all of them to attack the demons, and snatched Aladana. She took to the air, while everyone attacked the demons. She said confidently to Aladana, "This time, we're one step ahead of you." Aladana left, "I'm so sad as that feeling is short-lived."

Totally unexpected, fire came out of Aladana's mouth like one from a dragon. Isabella was pushed back and was luckily saved from the steaming fire. She said in disbelief, "I thought you were a Light", "I can't share everything. I already gave too much," Aladana interrupted. Suddenly, Sachel appeared out of nowhere, placed a device on Miss A's head and disappeared. The next moment, Aladana was plummeting from the sky. Isabella raced down to save her but she was held back by Sachel and was teleported with her. She and Isabella landed on the ground. All the students and demons stopped fighting to see what had turned out to be tragic. Aladana's dead, bleeding body was crushed on the ground. The four of them - not including Sachel - were thinking 'It didn't have to end that way.'

CHAPTER FIFTEEN

ONE ENEMY DOWN, ONE TO GO

The four of them dragged Sachel into a corner, red-faced. Sachel realised quite late why everyone was staring at her in a mad, indiginant way. Before they could shower her with insults, she started with her explanation; saying that she used the opportunity effectively. In a way, she was right. It was Aladana's fault for not being conscious of her surroundings, and in a game where no one can be trusted, letting down your guard is too big of a blunder to be called a mistake. Sachel went on to say that the five of them had gotten themselves into a dangerous game: where there is no way out once you have started playing, and that they had to be ruthless to survive.

Reluctantly, they nodded their heads. They had to move on. While one of their enemies was eliminated, they still had to wipe out one more. The perfect idea struck them. With the proof they had gathered, they could take it to the Board Of Mysains. While they had stood with Aladana in her plans to destroy Earth, they were clueless about her plans to overthrow them. That would at least delay their plans, if not change their minds.

Ignoring Sachels' eye rolls, they all nodded towards each other in affirmation of the plan. Before they could proceed, Surlay revealed his suspicion about Miffina. Despite being on Aladana's side for so long, how could she have come to their side with such short notice? Myran imitated Isabella's death stare towards Surlay, but it seemed as though it did not have any effect on him. Isabella however, defended Miffina's claim that Aladana had her controlled under a chip, which most likely led to her betraying them. Myran nodded almost too firmly, giving him an acute neck ache. Miffina's face was expressionless.

The theory was believable, however, Surlay was convinced they should do a twenty-four-hour surveillance on Miffina just to be safe and not take her to the upcoming Board meeting. It sounded reasonable. Even Myran couldn't argue. Miffina was angry to say the least, as she didn't understand the need for such extreme measures. She pointed out that she could be a valuable asset in the meeting, and that they needed her there with them. Out of all the people, Myran stepped up, and emotionally explained to his sister the whole situation. All Miffina did was grunt but later on she nodded.

Leaving this all aside, they still hadn't answered one vital question. How were they going to get a meeting fixed with the board? They certainly had not created such a great impact on the board in their last meeting as they were hoping to. They had sent a message that they were against the Board's thought of destroying Earth. So they couldn't ask for a direct meeting. Danzella was still the receptionist and the last person to let them in or meet the board.

Nevertheless, they could try Danzella. There wouldn't be any harm in trying so, for she could only say NO. If Aladana could say yes, they couldn't see why Danzella couldn't. The common thing they observed between Danzella and Miss A was that both would show their ease when they had the upper hand. It didn't always work for them, but in this case, it would have.

They shared their plan with Sachel. She found it well thought of though she made one request. She wanted to come with the four of them. Sachel believed that she had to make a stand. Everyone blamed her for what happened in the past when it was her creation's fault, for which she had no intent. Staying hidden was not an option. She had to show herself, show who she was. While all of them found it inspiring and true, they explained to her that they couldn't take the chance, especially not in such an important meeting. They promised her that she would have a chance, just not then.

Grumbling, Sachel stormed out of the room. Immediately, the four of them left the room and headed off to Sementrem Slackery. Sachel called her driver to drop them off, although she was not pleased. All of them hopped in. Within a few hours, they reached the grand hall doors of the colossal palace-like structure. It seemed as though they had made quite a few renovations. Large signs of a ball were hung up everywhere. Curiously, they all got off and instead of heading straight to Danzella, they diverted their path to the one that was decorated extravagantly- a slightly longer route to the reception.

There were still lots of people hanging up the decorations, so they couldn't see much, however, it was beautifully lit. As they continued forward, the number of people and decorations that were put up reduced. What was once a bustling hall, became a desolate alley. Curiously, they travelled forward. To their astonishment, they found themselves inside a dimly lit, old room. Spiderwebs hung from the ceiling while the floor remained broken and cracked. It looked as if a fight had occurred.

Councillor Iliria was hiding behind a table in the corner. Sensing something wrong, they silently walked towards Iliria, asking her what happened. She froze and could neither utter a word nor blink. The moment they thought of her being in coma, she started wailing and weeping in short but loud outbursts of tears.

After a long time, she calmed herself down and settled. Gently, they reposed their question to the councillor. Gathering herself together, she explained, "Danzella came in the Board Room to inform us about Aladana. We were surprised about her ambitions. As a result, we put a tag on Danzella for she was closest to Miss A, and could have been working with her. However, she found the tracker and destroyed it. When she asked us about it, we were here, decorating our room and as we were explaining why we did it, she showed her dark side and took away all the councillors. I hid behind the table so that she couldn't find me."

Unfortunately, Illiria had no clue where Danzella was headed. All three of them had a terrible idea. If Danzella took all the councillors, she would probably collect all of those who were suspicious or knew about her betrayal and do something to torment them. She would probably go after Sachel as she knew her hideout. The three of them took Illiria and told her to be with Miffina. It would also prove to be a test of whether Miffina was on their side.

Isabella offered to stand by if any mishap occurred, while Surlay and Myran went to Sachel's house. By the time they reached, Danzella was already at the door. She turned around, enraged at the sight of both the boys. Growling like a monster, she tore through the door and entered the house, vandalising everything. She scratched all the furniture like a cat and turned the whole place upside-down in search of Sachel. Bolting towards the door, they tried following Danzella in a quest to stop her. Danzella couldn't find Sachel and nor could the boys. They were determined to find her before Danzella did. Unfortunately, Danzella realised that the boys were following her.

She was steaming with rage. Surprisingly, she didn't bother chasing them. Dropping one's guard down could be fatal when face-to-face with an enemy. That was a mistake that the two boys did. Suddenly, Myran's eyes opened. He tried getting up but was unable to. He realised that his legs were tied with a rope and his arm chained above his head. He looked around, but could not see anyone. He was enclosed in a room with walls scratched like a cat. The chandelier hung gloomily from the pierced ceiling through which the fragmented pieces of light glimmered.

He adjusted himself into a reasonably comfortable position and used his light strike to cut through the ropes. Vigilantly, he crept past the intricate statues that were mounted on the stools in the hall in front of him. Sweating with fear, he climbed a staircase through which multiple sounds were echoing. He peeped furtively making sure his presence was unnoticed. Owing to the boisterous waves, he figured they were on a ship.

His eyes unveiled a horrific scene. Miffina was consulting with Danzella, laughing heartily. No extent of partiality could forgive this treacherousness. Surlay, who was being guarded by Rovendy, was tied to a pillar trying to scream for help. Right before he was going to take a stand, his mobile phone started buzzing exposing his position. Hastily, he declined the call. However, it was too late. Both the girls had heard the sound. They immediately got up and ran towards Myran. He had to escape: it was his only option. However, he couldn't leave Sulray to rot in their hands. This was also perhaps his first and last opportunity to save Rovendy from Danzella.

He dashed in the direction through which he came and banked right. He noticed that Danzella and Miffina covered both sides to cut him off. If he was to lose them, he had to play this smartly. He shot light beams in the opposite direction to which they were running as a diversion. The minute they followed the light, Myran shot off towards Surlay. He stunned Rovendy from afar and started untying Surlay's ropes. Myran questioned, "What's going on?" Surlay shakily replied, "It's just as Danzella said. She's rounding up all those who are conspiring against her. Miffina appeared out of nowhere and offered her assistance. I am clueless about how she escaped Isabella."

Myran realised that Isabella must have been in trouble. He quickly untied Surlay and told him to keep Rovendy occupied. Myran had to get to Isabella. He took out the transportation device that Aladana had given them on their first day of university and headed off. He found her wounded in a dark alleyway, struggling for breath. She had a vertical cut on her throat covering her neck in dark-red ink. Scrupulously, he lifted her and ran to the hospital.

The hospital was bustling with patients and doctors, screaming and shrieking. He manoeuvred his way through the crowd and reached the desolate emergency room. He placed her on the bed and went to fetch some doctors. Within a few minutes, a group of doctors and nurses swarmed into the room, preparing for the operation. Myran inquired if Isabella was going to be okay. The doctor commented that it was too early to say; however, he was not hopeful. The wound was deep and she suffered a lot of blood loss.

Myran knew Isabella for a long time and knew she would get through this. Meanwhile, he had some other matters to attend to. He teleported back to the ship and found it deserted and bleak. Shards of glass were scattered around the floor like a torn carpet. Something fishy was going on. Holding his guard up, he progressed forward, ready to face anything. He heard a cacophony of noises reverberating throughout the hallway. He started tracing the source of the noise which led him to a pitch-black dark room. His eyes seemed to have been deceiving him.

CHAPTER SIXTEEN

REVIVING AND REDIVIDING

Surlay was rummaging through the drawers, while papers were taking flight in the air. Right before Myran could ask a question, Surlay raised his hand and continued with his messy search. Myran chose a cosy corner and sat on the floor. Surlay seemed to have found what he was looking for as he was dancing like a wild chicken. He turned towards Myran to share his happiness but immediately noticed Myran's gloomy face. Before he could ask what was wrong, Myran told, "Isabella has a deep wound. The doctors are not hopeful."

Surlay sat next to him and kept his hand on his shoulder. He told him exactly the opposite of what he was thinking. Surlay explained, "It's okay to feel downcast. I am crestfallen. It's a natural feeling. Isabella is one of us. If she goes, our whole world will go down the drain. But sulking around isn't going to help. We need to stop them. That's what she would want from us."

Feeling slightly better, Myran questioned what he was dancing about. He replied that he discovered that Danzella was keeping Rovendy under a spell. He had found the antidote and was about to deliver it to him. He had also sent Miffina and Danzella on a wild goose chase; they wouldn't be back for a long time. Myran nodded. Cautiously, Surlay injected the antidote inside Rovendy. For a few seconds, nothing happened. Suddenly, his body swung upward and hit the ceiling hard. Smash! He fell on the floor and started rubbing his head. Realising the grogginess that Rovendy was experiencing, they picked him up and put him on the bed so that he could get some rest.

All of a sudden, a pungent odour was wafting through the room. They realised it was stun gas. They tried sprinting out of the room with Rovendy. Miffina stood near the entrance of the door, impeding their path. Her face was painted with anxiety as she dropped down, begging for mercy and forgiveness. Gently, they lifted her and asked her what happened.

She explained she had gone undercover to take down Danzella. She plotted it with Isabella. Danzella arrived where both of them were, so she had to hurt Isabella to make it seem realistic. At the moment, it was hard to trust anyone. However, they needed all the help they could find. They questioned, "What's the plan?" She pointed towards the exit. They had to leave immediately. Frantically, they all dashed out of the room - hauling Rovendy with them.

They had to wait for Rovendy to regain consciousness, as dragging him everywhere would only slow them down. They couldn't wait long, or else it would be too late. Myran enquired about the location of Danzella. He also asked about the location of the councillors and if anyone else was captured. Miffina replied, "I told Danzella to flee to our house, as I figured we could ambush her there. The councillors are in Sementrum Slacker. They are enclosed in a tiny, claustrophobic room near the Board Room. No one else was captured. Before you ask about Sachel, she managed to escape."

Just as Miffina finished her explanation, Rovendy started breathing heavily: as if he was grasping for breath. Immediately, both of them surrounded him in an attempt to comfort him. He got up - seeming a little dizzy - and started muttering gibberish. Myran asked about the medicine that Surlay administered to Rovendy. He said he had found a paper for an antidote written in Danzella's handwriting, so he used that.

Miffina put her hand on her head, explaining that the antidote was a set-up as Danzella realised that if they found Rovendy, you would try to heal him. Surlay had given him the wrong concoction. Luckily, Miffina knew the formula, but she stated thatsthe ingredients were inside the collapsed base with rubble protecting it from all sides. Danzella exclusively developed them.

Myran insisted that he would stay and collect the items, while Surlay and Miffina could go to the house to at least keep her busy. Surlay - knowing the potential of the Mylia Twins - suggested both of them to go. He was still skeptical where Miffina's loyalties lied. It wasn't reassuring that she kept on changing sides. However, he knew that they couldn't stop Danzella without her help. Dropping his lips into a pout, he promised Myran that he wouldn't mix anything up. Handing over the formula, they nodded with confidence and teleported into thin air.

CHAPTER SEVENTEEN

TWO-WAY BATTLE

Surlay unscrolled the paper and read it as if it were a document. He couldn't make out any names due to the horrendous handwriting. Nevertheless, there were well-drawn diagrams to help him identify the items. He needed to collect them as fast as possible, as the Mylia Twins would eventually need his assistance. All the ingredients had to be in the lab where Danzella used to make everything. He needed to find the lab.

Sweating profusely, he navigated through the rubble and located the lab. It was in ramshackle. Broken pieces of glass were scattered on the floor. Cautiously, he tip-toed his way to the vandalised table. Most of the bottles were intact. Their worn-off labels didn't help much, nor did Miffina's elaborate drawings, as none mimicked the one she drew.

Nevertheless, there was a solution. Miffina had noted down the salts present in each of the medicines. They weren't rare and were readily available. He stood resolute that he would be able to concoct the medicine. The first item on the list was Craspanastian. It could be created by mixing thunder with a six-leaved clover. The clovers were in abundance around the tottering parts of the building.

He could bring thunder, however, he couldn't control the placement of the lightning. He had to be careful because one strike could wipe out whatever remained. He started gathering the clouds with some peculiar movements of his hands. As the cotton-like clouds drifted together, they clashed like two gods in a fierce battle. Booming sounds filled the room. He sprinted outside towards the clover patch. Gently plucking one, he raised his hand proudly, waiting for lightning to grace it with its presence.

Nothing happened for a few dramatic minutes. Hopelessness drained his face's colour. Grumbling in disappointment, he took a few steps back. Suddenly lightning struck the building. It started dancing and rocking about in madness. Frantically, he stuffed all the bottles he could find in a bag and dashed out of the building. It steadily collapsed but crash-landed in the end, spreading dust everywhere.

He had to hurry up. If he continued at this pace, he would never be done. He was desperate for the lightning to have a little mercy and hit the clover. Just as the words slipped out of his mouth, the lightning embraced the clover with its sting. Jumping frivolously, he opened the paper and read the next ingredient.

Meanwhile, Surlay managed to complete his task by the hair, The Mylia Twins were struggling. They made their way to the house, however, they could not find Danzella. Scouting the place cautiously, they inspected every corner and left no stone unturned. It seemed like Danzella figured it was a trap and managed to escape. "Do you think she escaped?" Myran questioned.

Miffina seemed to be confused. Shaking her head, she pointed out, "It's unlikely. I bet she is hiding somewhere. She trusts me, and so would obey me. She is a natural at hiding." Nodding, both of them continued to search. They had to start thinking like Danzella and get inside her head. It was likely that she could have been hiding in their battleground due to the numerous cubby spaces and hiding spots.

They decided it was best for Miffina to call out for her and to keep her unaware of Myran's presence. Miffan's voice reverberated throughout the hall. Steadily, they lurched closer towards the battleground. Suddenly, Danzella announced in a booming voice, "I'm aware you're with Myran. I've been tracking you this whole time. Why did you betray me? We could have done so many things together. You had great potential, and it's not too late to return to me"

Myran placed his hands on his sister's shoulder. He persuaded her that Danzella was luring her into a trap she could never escape. Yelling in frustration, she pulled away from Myran but didn't even inch closer to Danzella. She felt controlled as if she was some pawn in a game. Seclusion was dawning upon her. Everyone was pointing out what was right and wrong and the lines between the two worlds were becoming blurred.

She could not confess her feelings to herself because she didn't know what they were. Anger? A feeling of betrayal? A shower of Indignance? Her brain couldn't take all of this in. She would mostly walk out of the room, saying she needed time. However, at that time, it wasn't an option. Most people say to make your option, however, it wasn't the case here. She had to pick a side.

Putting everything aside together, she pulled her head together and tried pondering: what did she think? Slowly and steadily, she crept towards Myran with surprising ease. She had made up her mind. The same successive story could have been similarly said for Surlay, as he managed to collect and make all the ingredients required. In a hurried manner, he fed the antidote to Rovendy. He immediately fell asleep, which was a sign of success. Miffina had mentioned in the scroll that this was a sign of recovery. He was ready to help the Twins.

Just before he was about to teleport himself to them, he decided to check on Isabella first. The Twins could surely have waited a little longer. He quickly disappeared into thin air. Upon reaching the hospital, a doctrine of doctors were rushing towards the emergency room. Furtively, he followed the doctors to the room, which confirmed his greatest fear.

Isabella's situation had worsened. Her heart rate plummeted severely. He knew he couldn't leave her in this situation, however, he couldn't leave the Mylia twins. They finally found Danzella, and it was their chance to exact their revenge. Mumbling a sincere apology, he teleported himself to the house. Stealthily, he tip-toed his way around the house in search of any action.

"Ah! Who's there?" screamed Surlay and the Twins as they bumped into each other. They swiftly turned around and were about to use their powers against each other when they realised it was only them. Sighing with relief, Myran questioned about the antidote. Giving an affirmative nod, Surlay mentioned that Rovendy was on a path of recovery. He decided not to mention Isabella, as it would only distract Myran and make him worried sick.

"Ahem? I'm still here," Danzella reminded. Surlay was surprised that they just started talking to him instead of capturing her, but who was to blame them? Awkwardly turning around, they smiled. Suddenly, Miffina hurled a dark ball at Danzella, hoping to have an element of surprise.

However, her hope was thrown away in the gutter as she deflected it with ease. "You're going to have to do a lot more than that to capture me," Danzella laughed with a hint of smugness.

Smiling all three of them quickly surrounded her and started attacking with all of their offensive powers. Danzella seemed to be struggling, but it was not enough. She claimed she was stronger than three untrained college students. However, that was where she was wrong. They protected Earth from so many attacks. They knew what to do, but Danzella knew more. She was much more experienced.

Out of the blue, Rovendy appeared and helped in the fight against Danzella. In the absolute shock of his appearance, Danzella let down her guard. Taking advantage of the situation, they attacked with full force. Danzella was pushed backwards and lay unconscious. "She is just a little struck by the attack. She will come back to her senses in an hour or so," Miffina explained.

Realising that Rovendy had just popped out of nowhere, they started bombarding him with questions. He still should have been asleep, and they were confused about how he knew their location. He replied, "I figured you guys might have wanted to stop Danzella. While I don't remember much about my talks with her, I do remember Miffina telling her to flee the house, so I thought I should come to help. I figured you might be needing some."

After everyone got reacquainted with each other, they caged Danzella and decided to have a look at Isabella. Taking a deep breath, they teleported themselves to the hospital.

CHAPTER EIGHTEEN

A New Beginning

Taking quick steps, they rushed to the emergency room to see Isabella. She was still on the medical bed, wrapped cosily in a blanket. Her eyes were closed as if she was sleeping. Slowly lifting her hand, she asked softly, "Did we win?" They all nodded. A soft smile appeared on her face. She whispered, "Could I talk to Myran alone?" Everyone left the room with a suppressed nod.

Myran was quite surprised. Maybe she wanted to talk about something serious. She said in a worried voice, "We need to be ready. I highly doubt we have eradicated all of her enemies. Danzella has a lot of contacts. I heard it during their conversation when Miffina had stabbed me. She had a lot of contacts. Danzella also mentioned that if she ever died, she told all of her horrendous friends to carry on her legacy and destroy us."

Myran seemed curious. What Isabella was saying, didn't add up. When he found her, she was lying unconscious on the floor. How could she have possibly heard it? Her wound was also fresh, and so he wasn't late to attend her. He decided to ask his questions slowly and strategically.

"Did you hear anything after that?" he asked. She replied that she had only heard that much. He also questioned the duration of Danzella's conversation. She answered, "It was about ten minutes long. She took a long time to say it and elaborated a lot." Myran went straight to the point. "How did you hear the ten-minute-long conversation when you told me you only heard one line?"

A smug appeared on Isabella's face. "You caught me." Suddenly, she grabbed her face and started ripping it off, revealing it was just a mask. It was Danzella! He couldn't believe it. It was impossible. They had Danzella caged up with them. He rushed towards the cage where he saw Dazella. Or supposedly, a copy of her. Suddenly, she started cackling evilly as she transformed into someone who they thought they had gotten rid of: ALADANA!

Myran opened his mouth in disbelief. "Did you think you could get rid of me? I'm a shapeshifting demon myself," announced Aladana. Myran questioned, "What did you do with Isabella? Where is she?" Aladana replied that she was in their secret chamber far away from everywhere. Just as Myran was about to leave, Aladana warned, "Be careful. Our game has only just begun."

www.ingramcontent.com/pod-product-compliance
Lightning Source LLC
Chambersburg PA
CBHW031452130726
47989CB00003B/1354